# My Fox Ate My Report Card

David Blaze

This book is a work of fiction. Names, characters, places, and incidents are the product of the author's imagination or are used factiously. Any resemblance to actual events, locales, or persons, living or dead, is coincidental.

For Zander…

Wow! That's Awesome!

# CONTENTS


Friday Morning 1

Friday Afternoon 6

Friday Night 15

Saturday Morning 23

Saturday Afternoon 29

Saturday Night 35

Sunday Morning 42

Sunday Afternoon 46

Sunday Night 52

Monday Morning 57

Monday Afternoon 63

Monday Evening 74

## FRIDAY MORNING

I smashed a handful of clay on the table in front of me with a bang. Every kid in the art class stared at me. The past few months had been hard without Fox. My grades in school had slipped and I hadn't even realized it. At least not until I got my report card in Miss Cox's class earlier.

Sam hovered over my shoulder. "You're supposed to be the smart one," he said. He must have seen my report card on the table, because he shouted, "Hey, everyone! Joe got a C in English!" He reached around me, snatched it, and held it up for the class to see.

"Pipe down!" Miss Pendleton shouted. She was the oldest teacher at school. She wore a long skirt that went up past her waist and to her chest. She glared at us from her desk.

I grabbed the report card from Sam. He wore his

usual tank top to show off his biceps. He laughed at me and returned to the group at his art table across the room. He high fived one of them.

"No Mama, nooo!" Sam shouted in a high-pitched voice. The class laughed. He looked around and smirked. He slammed his own handful of clay on his table. "I didn't mean to get a bad grade! Please don't hurt me!"

The class kept laughing. I could only shake my head. He picked up the clay and slammed it down again and again onto the tabletop. It sounded like a kid getting spanked with a wooden spoon. The class laughed louder and louder until Miss Pendleton shouted, "Knock it off!"

Melissa bumped her shoulder against mine. "Hey, Joe. Don't listen to him." She put a thumb down. I loved her smile and bouncy ponytails. I smiled back and nodded.

"English is my best class," I told her. "I write for the school newsletter." I tapped my fingers on the table. "I don't know how I'm going to tell my mom about this."

Melissa waved her hands at me. "I didn't pass Math. Remember?" She bit her lower lip. "I'm the one going to summer school."

I nodded. "You win."

She chuckled. "It doesn't feel like it." She looked over my report card. "Show your mom. She'll understand." I wasn't sure about that.

"Do you like my flower pot?" Melissa asked. I couldn't tell her the truth. Melissa didn't have any artistic talent with clay. Her flower pot looked like a soccer ball had exploded.

"It's beautiful," I lied.

She smiled. "It's for my dad," she said.

Sam came by our table again and laughed his head off. "Your dad likes flowers?" He shook his head. "Real men don't like flowers." He made sure to stop by every student and tell them about Melissa's dad.

Melissa shrugged her shoulders at me. "My dad likes to keep fresh roses. They were my mom's favorite." She rubbed her eyes. "Stupid allergies."

Before I could say anything, Miss Pendleton tapped me on the shoulder. I gulped. She was not a nice person when she was mad. All I could see was her skirt when I turned to face her. It was as high as my head.

"Tell me that you're done, Jonah," she said. Her arms were crossed. "I've got to get this work in the kiln tonight."

The rest of the school called me Joe. No matter how many times I reminded Miss Pendleton that I didn't like being called Jonah, she still forgot. I wondered how old she was. "It'll be a minute or two," I assured her.

"Well, what are you making?" she asked. "A salad bowl?" She flinched like she was disgusted. "I hate salads!"

I looked at my work and had to agree — it did look like a big salad bowl. But that's not what it was. "I need more time," I told her. "It has to be perfect."

She squeezed her eyes and shouted, "Look at me! Look at me! Do I look like I'm getting any younger?"

"No!" Sam shouted from across the room. The class laughed with him again.

Miss Pendleton waved her fists like a crazy person. "That just burns me up!" She marched to her desk, huffing and puffing with every step.

Melissa nudged me. "I like salad." She smirked. "Taco salad!"

I tried not to laugh because, well, it wasn't funny. "You've been hanging around the cat too much," I told her. She laughed hysterically.

"I'm a Meow Master," she mocked, chopping her arms in the air like a karate expert. I laughed with her. PJ had kept our lives interesting while Fox was gone. Crazy cat.

I looked at the clock on the wall behind Miss Pendleton. Five minutes were left in class. I stared at my report card as I put it into my backpack. I wasn't sure I could give it to my mom. But that wasn't my greatest fear.

I needed to see Fox so he could give me an update. He and his parents had been searching our land and the forest. Something dark was coming. They were doing whatever they could to keep it away from us.

## FRIDAY AFTERNOON

I jumped into my Uncle Mike's pickup truck in the school parking lot. My little cousin Dana was in the middle seat. She smirked at me and punched my arm. I flinched. She was a lot stronger than she thought she was.

"Play nice," my uncle warned. He turned from the steering wheel and winked at me. "She's a sweet little kid." Sure, a sweet little kid with the strength of a rhino!

"You'll be okay," Dana taunted me. "Cry quietly in the corner." She burst out laughing. I rubbed my shoulder and shook my head. It was a good thing she was family and I liked her.

"How did you do on your report card?" my uncle asked.

I gulped. "I did okay."

He nodded and smiled at me. "Of course you did. You're the smartest kid I know." He pulled out of the parking lot.

"Hey!" Dana shouted. "What about me?" She crossed her arms.

My uncle cleared his throat. "I mean he's the second smartest kid I know." He looked straight ahead.

I sat back and closed my eyes. It was a thirty-minute trip out of town to the wildlife sanctuary. I hadn't been there in a while but was ready to get back to work. I couldn't wait for summer. I could be there with the animals all day.

Something jumped into my lap and slapped me in the face with a wet tongue. I screamed. My eyes shot open. Fox's bright blue eyes stared back at me.

"Fox!" I shouted. I wrapped my arms around him. His brown and orange fur was warm and comforting. "What are you doing here?" I looked behind the seat and realized he had been hiding there.

"Chinese sneak attack!" he said in his childish voice. He licked my face again. I laughed with him and Dana.

"Miss Julie wants to see Fox," my uncle said.

I didn't know why she wanted to see him. Fox was as healthy as an ox. Hey, that rhymes! I held him closer. Fox had been through way too much in the last year. I hoped there was nothing wrong with him.

"Don't worry," Dana said. Her eyes were wide like everything was fine. I was glad she was there. "I won't tell your friends that I slap you around." She was being playful and having fun. At least I hope that's what she was doing.

"We're getting close," my uncle said. He nodded at me. "Dana will help you today and Fox will… do whatever he does."

Fox faced my uncle. "Don't make me bring the pain, Mary. Do not unleash Mr. Awesome Muscles."

My uncle stopped the pickup truck in front of the animal sanctuary. He turned to Fox. "My name isn't Mary."

Fox wiped a paw across his lips. "It will be when I'm done with you." Dana high fived him. Fox had learned a lot from her. Too much.

My uncle narrowed his eyes. "Sunday afternoon. You and me on the mat." I rolled my eyes. Fox and my uncle loved to watch wrestling on TV. Last week they dressed like wrestlers. Fox wore bright red underwear. It was ridiculous.

I hopped out of the truck with Fox and Dana. I didn't bother to tell Dana that I was in charge once we got inside the sanctuary. That never went over well. I jumped when my uncle honked his horn.

"Be good," he shouted out his window. "Give Fox a bath. He smells like pickles!" My uncle laughed and drove off.

Fox stood on his hind legs, sniffed his armpits and shuddered. "He's right. Don't stand too close."

I wasn't prepared for what I saw when we walked into the sanctuary. Animals were in cages all over the floor. Squirrels, opossum, rabbits, raccoons — too many to count! They were laid out like they were injured or worse. Miss Julie ran around the room, shouting into her cell phone. She closed it when she saw us.

"Come in, kids," she said, out of breath. "Go into the back and find as many cages as you can. We're going to need all of them."

Dana grabbed my hand as we looked over the animals. None of them were moving. "What's wrong with them?"

Fox sniffed at their cages. He looked at me and Miss Julie with sad eyes. "We have to help them."

Miss Julie focused her eyes on me. "You haven't been here in a while." She was right. When Fox had returned to his parents in the forest, I didn't want to be around the other animals. They reminded me of him.

"Christopher has been bringing in animals like this for more than a week," she continued. She and my mom called him Christopher, but I would always remember him as Tater the Exterminator. "They've been shot." She turned her head away from us. "I haven't been able to save all of them."

"I don't understand," I said. "Fox and his parents have been watching the forest. They were supposed to warn us." I looked at him. "How did you miss this?"

Miss Julie held out a hand. " It's not their fault. The Conecuh National Forest is 84,000 acres. It reaches from here to Florida." She shrugged. "There's no way Fox and his parents could watch all of it."

Dana let go of my hand. She put her arms around Fox. "You can't go back into the forest. You can't."

"Elan is flying here in a couple of days," Miss Julie said. "He's visiting his brother in Los Angeles." I gulped. The American Indian had warned my family that darkness was coming.

"An old friend wants to see you," Miss Julie said to Fox. He was standing on his hind legs. He put his paws in the air like he was confused.

Miss Julie's face softened. "Christopher found a young skunk a few weeks ago. He's your age." Fox's ears perked up. "He has a broken paw, but it's healing much faster than I expected." She smiled for the first time that afternoon. "He reminds me of you."

A kid skunk stepped into the room on hind legs, just like Fox! He looked around at us with bright blue eyes then stared at Fox. "Don't pull your dad's finger!" he shouted.

Fox ran right past me and tackled the skunk. They jumped around each other and laughed like they were old friends.

"Who is that?" Dana asked me. I shrugged, wondering the same thing myself.

"This is my friend Stinky!" Fox shouted. He wrapped an arm around the skunk and chuckled.

Dana crossed her arms. "Why is his name Stinky?"

Fox and Stinky burst out laughing. "Don't ask," Fox advised.

The front door opened behind us. Tater the Exterminator walked in with another cage in his hand. A rabbit was laid out in it. "Where should I put this one?" he asked. That's when he saw me and Dana. "Oh, hey kids."

I barely recognized him. He had lost a lot of weight and combed his hair over his forehead. I remembered him as a chubby man with a huge forehead and a hotdog nose. At least he still had the nose. You could see it from a mile away.

Dana shrunk away from him and stood close to my side. We would never forget the day he had barged into my house and taken Fox away. He had changed since then. My mom trusted him, so I trusted him too.

"What are we going to do?" Miss Julie asked Tater. "We're running out of room." Her voice was weak. Her shoulders were low.

Tater shrugged. "It's déjà vu." Miss Julie nodded. Tater stared at Fox. "The same thing happened last year when your parents were shot."

Miss Julie cried. She cleared her throat and said, "I'm sorry."

"It's got to be the same hunters," Tater continued. He put a hand on his forehead. "It doesn't make any sense, though. They're not taking the animals. They're leaving them."

Fox and Stinky whispered to each other. When they were done, Fox looked at me and raised his chin. That meant he wanted my attention later. He didn't want Tater to know. Fox was afraid of him.

"It's like they want to wipe out all the animals in the forest," Tater said. He shook his head and set the cage down. His face was creased and red.

"They're looking for something specific," Miss Julie said. "And they're not going to stop until they find it." She waved her hands like she had no idea what to do. "Elan will have answers," she assured us.

I hoped Miss Julie was right about Elan and wrong about everything else. Somehow the hunters knew Fox wasn't the only creature with blue eyes that could walk and talk.

# FRIDAY NIGHT

It was quiet at the kitchen table. My mom sat at one end and my uncle sat at the other. Dana sat across from me. Fox searched the refrigerator for any leftover chicken. PJ was taking a nap. I used to think he was lazy, but cats sleep up to twenty hours a day.

"Let's see your report card, Jonah," my mom said. She rubbed her hands together and smiled like she was excited. When we first moved to Alabama, grades dropped because I missed a lot of school. I got straight A's on the last report card.

Thunder roared outside. I hoped I wasn't going to be struck by lightning. "I left it in my locker," I said. "I'm sorry. I'll get it Monday." Her eyes narrowed. I had to change the subject. "What are we going to do about the animals?"

She leaned back and crossed her arms. I wished I could read her mind. I hoped she believed me. "I can't believe someone's hurting them." She shook her head and huffed. A vein in her forehead looked like it was ready to explode.

"Pass the salt, please," my uncle said. He rubbed his hands together. My mom had made his favorite dinner — pork chops and french fries. He had the last porkchop. This was his third helping. My mom glared at him. "What?" he asked. "I said please."

The refrigerator door slammed shut. Fox came to the table and sat next to me. "All I ask for is a little chicken," he complained. He stared at my uncle's plate. "That looks good."

My uncle pulled his plate closer. "Salt? Please pass the salt?"

"I don't want it anyways," Fox said. "It doesn't taste like chicken."

Dana laughed. "How would you know? You don't eat pork chops."

Fox leaned across the table and winked at my uncle. "I licked it earlier."

My uncle looked down at his plate. "Never mind. Keep the salt." He pushed his plate forward and stared at Fox. I had a feeling the wrestling match between Fox and my uncle was going to be epic. I'd have to get a front row seat.

I raise my chin to Fox. He had wanted my attention earlier at the sanctuary. "What were you and Stinky talking about?" The skunk looked like his foot was better, but Miss Julie wanted to keep him for two more days. She was concerned about infection.

Fox nodded at me. "I've always been able to talk and walk on two legs." He spoke slowly. "I've done it since the first time I stepped out of my parents' den."

"You don't have to be a show off," Dana said. "I can rub my belly and pat my head at the same time." And that's what she did.

"He's not showing off," I said. I realized what Fox was telling us. I looked into his blue eyes. "You didn't get your powers from my great-grandmother's land like Elan thought. They came from somewhere else."

"The forest," my mom whispered. "I should have seen it. There could be more like you." We already knew of two animals like him.

Fox nodded. "My family was hunted by two men." He stared at the wall across from us. "Stinky saved me."

I grabbed his arm to get his attention. "The hunters. It's the same men leaving the injured animals behind today, isn't it?" I could see in his eyes the answer was yes.

My uncle stood. "This is good. We can work with this." He put his hands on the table. "What did they look like?"

Fox shrugged. "I only saw them from a

distance." He stared at his paws. "My parents buried me in the den." He looked at my uncle. "I didn't see them up close, but I heard them."

My uncle walked over to Fox and knelt next to him. "Think. What did they say?" His voice was high like he was frustrated.

Fox leaned away from him. "You need a breath mint." He waved a paw in front of his nose.

My uncle stood and grunted. "What did they say?" he repeated.

Fox looked at me. "Tater was right. They're hunting all of the animals in the forest."

My uncle threw his hands up and returned to his chair. "That doesn't help us," he complained. "We already knew that."

Fox pounded a paw on the table. "Hold on to your britches, Mary." He was talking to my uncle. "The names of the hunters are Billy and John. They're being paid a lot of money."

My mom smiled and cheered. "You're a smart fox!" I agreed with her. Fox remembered names he had only heard once. And he hadn't seen their faces.

My uncle fumed in his seat. "Who?" We looked at him, confused. "Who is paying them?"

"I don't know," Fox admitted. He stared at the wall across from us again. His face froze like he was lost in thought. "They said the boss was paying them a lot of money."

"The boss?" my mom asked. "That could be anyone. Do you guys know any hunters named Billy or John?" We shook our heads. "I'll check with Christopher. He knows a lot of hunters."

"It could be Chen," I said. "He could be the boss." I hoped I was wrong. The man from China had tried to kidnap Fox twice before.

I jumped when there was a knock on the front door. "Fox, go into the bedroom," my mom told him.

"I know the drill," he said. "I'll go mess with the cat. He hates it when I do that." Fox got out of his seat, went into the hall, then into my bedroom.

I went to the door with my mom. Shane was on the other side, standing in the rain when we opened it. He was the tallest kid at school but at least he finally stopped growing. Once my enemy, he was now my friend.

"Get in here," my mom told him. "You're soaking wet." He stood there, letting the rain fall on his head and shoulders.

"My dad…" he said, looking lost. "I didn't know how to tell you. I'm sorry." I was worried. I motioned for him to come in, but he shook his head.

"He got out of prison a few days ago," Shane continued, "but he didn't come home." I couldn't move. It was obvious who the boss was. Shane's dad, Mr. Connors, didn't know I had the same blue eyes as Fox. It happened after he went to prison. He didn't know what I could do. He couldn't find out. He was far too dangerous.

"Get in here," my mom said again. She grabbed his arm and pulled him inside. "I'm not going to let you get sick." She pointed to the hall. "My brother has some spare clothes in the guest bedroom. Go dry off and put them on." He was way too tall to fit into my clothes.

My mom went back into the kitchen with me. "Charles Connors is out of prison," she told my uncle before she sat down.

"Mystery solved," he said. 'We need to figure out a plan." He took a deep breath. "I'm sorry for earlier," he said to Fox. "You've been a big help."

"No problem," Fox said. "I'm sorry I called you Mary." He smiled. "And I'm sorry I lied. I didn't lick your porkchop."

"What?" my uncle asked. He pulled his plate close again. "Salt? Please pass the salt?"

## SATURDAY MORNING

I glanced at the man standing at the table next to us. He had a brown beard and mustache. My mom and I had been coming to the farmers market for a year. Mr. Jim Bob had always been at that table with his fruits and vegetables. This didn't feel right. Where was Mr. Jim Bob?

"Good morning!" the stranger shouted to us with a smile. He walked around his table and came over to our table full of eggs. He wore a brown leather belt with the biggest buckle I had ever seen. It was silver with the image of a cowboy holding his hat in the air while riding a horse.

"Good morning," my mom said. "It's nice to see a new face." She reached out a hand and shook his.

"I'm Julie." She wrapped an arm around me. "This is my son Jonah."

I squeezed out of her grip. "Joe," I told the man smiling at me. "My name is Joe."

"Joe," he whispered, crossing his arms. His smile disappeared. His eyes narrowed. "I've heard a lot about you."

I gulped. What had he heard? The last stranger who knew who I was had nearly destroyed my world. Was I in danger? I leaned against my mom and put her arm back around me.

"Uncle Max!" a familiar voice shouted from the crowd. I looked around the stranger and saw Melissa wearing sunglasses and with a drink in hand. She ran to the stranger and hugged him.

My fists tightened. I didn't know this man. I didn't trust him. What had he done to Mr. Jim Bob?

He pointed at me and shook his head. "So," he said to Melissa, "this is the guy you have a crush on?" Her face turned red. She covered her forehead with a hand. "What?" her uncle asked. "You talk about him all the time."

My mom chuckled in a way I hadn't heard in years. "It's nice to meet you, Max."

He winked at her. "I wanted to surprise my niece." He looked at the table next to ours and nodded. "I was talking to the guy running that table. We're both into airplanes." I'd never forget that crazy flight straight up into the air with Mr. Jim Bob. "He asked me to watch his table while he went to the restroom."

"You're not from around here, are you?" my mom asked. "You don't have a country accent like the rest of the city."

"He lives in Florida," Melissa said. She nudged him. "It must be nice to live in Orlando. You need to take me with you so I can go to Disney World."

"We're from Orlando!" my mom shouted. She took her arm from me again and walked around the table. "I love the sun and rain there. I miss the way the city lights up at night."

Mr. Max smiled. "I love it there." He looked into the crowd. "We could talk about it while we eat. Are you hungry?"

My mom chuckled again. "I could eat. They have hamburgers here." She motioned to me and Melissa. "Watch the tables. We'll bring you some food back." And just like that, she disappeared into the crowd with Melissa's uncle.

"That was weird," I said to Melissa. I didn't know what else to say to her. She talked about me all the time?

"Yeah," Melissa agreed. "Way weird." She smiled at me. "Did you show your mom your report card?"

I shuffled the eggs. "Not yet. I'm waiting for the right time."

"You should do it today," she said. She took off her sunglasses and set her drink down. "It's like pulling off a Band-Aid. It will sting a little at first, but you'll feel a lot better."

"Maybe," I said. I cut my knee once when I fell in a parking lot. It left a scar. It didn't hurt anymore, but it would be there for the rest of my life.

"How's my cat doing?" Melissa asked.

"PJ sleeps all day," I complained. "He only comes to life when you're around. You're his favorite person." Melissa liked to think of him as hers. I didn't mind. It was cool to have a talking cat, but I had been through so much with Fox. He was my best friend.

"You're a lot happier," she said. I wasn't sure what she meant. Happier than what? "Since Fox came back." I couldn't argue with her. I was lost when Fox had disappeared into the woods with his family for months. I couldn't lose him again.

"What's wrong, Joe?" she asked, standing between me and the eggs on the table. "You're quieter than usual."

I shrugged my shoulders. "It's silly." I couldn't shake the feeling that bad people were looking for me. Melissa put her hands in the air like she wanted me to tell her everything. I told her about the animals being hunted.

"That's not the worst part," I confided in her. "I don't want to be paranoid, but I think they're after me." I watched her eyes to see how she'd respond.

Melissa squinted her eyes like she was confused. Her face relaxed after a minute. "It's because you're like them, right? Fox and PJ?" I nodded. She tapped her chin with a finger. "Your eyes are bright blue like theirs. You're faster and stronger than you were before."

I nodded. "I feel like I'm being watched." I was embarrassed to admit it. I sounded like a crazy person. "I've got to find out who The Boss is."

"We've always stuck together," she said. "I won't let anything happen to you. They'll have to get through me first." She put her hands on her hips.

I believed her. I hoped I wasn't being paranoid. She winked at me and went to Mr. Jim Bob's table when a customer walked up to it.

That's when I froze. Two men in camouflage pants and jackets sat on a park bench in the middle of the crowd. They faced me and whispered to each other. They stood and walked away as soon as they realized I saw them.

I shook my head and took a deep breath. It had to be my imagination. No one was after me.

I wish I had been right.

## SATURDAY AFTERNOON

"Help!" Fox shouted from inside my house. "Somebody save me!"

I jumped out of the car and raced toward the house. I shouldn't have gone to the farmers market. I should have known better than to leave Fox in the house. Now he was in trouble and it was my fault.

"Jonah, wait!" my mom shouted after me. Her mouth was open, and her eyes begged me not to go. I couldn't wait. I had to save my friend.

"Don't hurt him!" Dana shouted at someone right before I shoved the front door open. Nobody better have touched Fox or my little cousin. I would give up everything to protect them. I was ready to do whatever I had to do.

I froze when I saw what was in front on me. My heart raced, and my chest was pounded. A large blue mat covered the living room floor. Dana and PJ were standing on the outside of it, staring at the two bodies wrestling in front of them. My Uncle Mike had Fox pinned on the mat.

"One!" Dana shouted. She banged her fist on the mat. "Two!" She banged it again.

"Come on, Fox!" PJ shouted. "We've gotta win! You can do it!"

Dana raised her hand to bang it one more time. But before she could, Fox opened his claws and scratched my uncle's hand.

"Ouch!" my uncle shouted, jumping back. He squeezed his hand a few times and stared at it. "That really hurt. You broke my skin." He shook his head and nodded at Dana. "It should be against the rules."

Fox stood and smirked. He turned his neck from side to side until it cracked. "There are no rules. My name is Captain Awesome Muscles, and this is war."

My mom rushed into the house behind me. "What's going on here?" she asked.

I turned and looked at her. "Children," I said, shaking my head. I got my breath back. "They're children."

My uncle grunted and pounced on Fox again. He

pinned my best friend to the mat like before. He turned his head away from Fox's armpits. "You still smell like pickles," he complained.

"I haven't had a bath this week," Fox admitted. He grinned and raised his armpits to my uncle's face. "Smell it! Smell it!"

Dana jumped down on the mat and banged her fist. "One!"

My mom closed the door behind her. "I'm going to make lunch," she said as she walked past me to the kitchen. "Any requests?"

"Chi…cken," Fox grunted. He stretched one of his paws out as far as he could while it was pinned. I couldn't understand why at first.

"Tag me in!" PJ shouted. "Come on! Come on!" He jumped up and down impatiently. Fox grimaced and reached out a little farther. Then it happened. PJ tapped his paw.

PJ jumped onto the mat on his two hind legs. He jumped from side to side, one leg to the other. "Gotta get the blood flowing," he said. He nodded at Fox as my best friend rolled out of the ring.

Fox noticed me for the first time and winked at me. I smiled at him and shrugged. A minute earlier I thought he was in danger. Thank goodness he wasn't. I would always do what I could to keep him safe.

Dana clasped her hands in front of her like she was holding a microphone. "Crazy Karate Cat steps into the ring," she announced. PJ put his paws together in front of him. It looked like he was praying. He bowed to my uncle like he was in a karate tournament.

"Let's see what you're made out of," my uncle said. He stood with his legs open wide and his hands in front of him. PJ didn't have a chance. All my uncle had to do was reach out and grab him. At least that's what I thought.

My uncle shot out his hands to grab PJ. At that very moment PJ did a somersault between my uncle's legs and ended up behind him. He turned to face my uncle's back and shouted, "Karate chop!" He threw a paw into the back of my uncle's leg like he had a black belt in karate.

My uncle fell to his knees and groaned. "Wow," I said. "PJ's gotten really good." Dana had been training him with what she learned in her karate classes. PJ had wanted to be good at karate. I didn't know he was serious about it.

PJ bowed to me. "Thank you, young grasshopper. I am a Meow Master."

My mom walked out of the kitchen and laughed. "I don't want to know what happened." She motioned to Dana. "Come help me set the table. Let's let the boys be boys."

Dana put her hands on her face and shook her head. "It's not my job," she whispered so my mom couldn't hear her. "You do it." What she didn't know was my mom could hear everything.

"I heard that, young lady," my mom said. She turned to my uncle. "Better get your daughter."

He stood and brushed his knees off. "Why? She reminds me of you at that age."

My mom chuckled. "I know. That's the problem."

PJ jumped from leg to leg again. "Are we doing this or not?" He punched his fists in front of him at an invisible punching bag.

"We're done here," my uncle said. He rubbed his knees. "I'm going to need some ice."

I watched him hobble into the kitchen. PJ and Fox went with him. They teased him a lot, but they respected him. I hoped I could be like my uncle one day.

What PJ had done was amazing. My uncle was much bigger than him. With one blow of PJ's paw, my uncle fell. I never thought I'd say it, but I'd be happy to have him by my side if we were in trouble.

That day was coming much sooner than I expected.

## SATURDAY NIGHT

Melissa and her uncle Max came to our house for dinner that night. My mom had invited them. Melissa's dad had returned to Puerto Rico for a few days. He was an electrician and wanted to make sure there weren't any more problems after Hurricane Irma last year.

"I'm glad you could join us," my mom said to Melissa. "I can't let you survive on burgers and tacos while your dad is gone." She winked at Mr. Max and led them into the kitchen.

"That's not fair," Mr. Max complained. "I do a lot more than order burgers and tacos." He winked back at my mom. "I also order pizza."

I was seated at the kitchen table with Dana and my Uncle Mike. "This is my brother Mike," my mom said, pointing to him. "And this is my niece Dana," she continued, pointing to her. "You already know Jonah. Go ahead and take a seat. Dinner will be ready in a minute."

"Joe," I reminded Mr. Max. "Please call me Joe."

He nodded at me. "You got it, Joe." He pulled out the chair next to mine. "I'll sit here." Dana was on the other side of the table. My uncle was at the end.

"Sit next to me," Dana said to Melissa. She patted the chair by hers. "Girl power." Melissa smiled at me and joined her.

My uncle stood and reached his arm past me. "It's nice to meet you," he said to Mr. Max. The man from Orlando shook his hand. "What do you do for a living?" He sat back down.

"I'm a writer," Mr. Max said. He had my full attention.

"Did you hear that, Jonah?" my mom asked. She opened the oven to check on the chicken she was baking. "He's a writer, too."

Mr. Max turned to me. "What do you write?" I wasn't sure how to answer him. I had sent articles to magazines, but none of them were published. My throat was dry, and my ears rang.

"He writes for the school newspaper," Melissa

said. She smiled at me again. "And he wrote an amazing paper about friendship." I mouthed the words 'thank you' to her.

My mom set a pan of baked barbecue chicken on the table. She came back with a big pot of mashed potatoes and another pot full of corn. "Help yourselves," she said as she sat at the other end of the table. "Make sure you save a piece for Fox."

Mr. Max raised his eyebrows. "Who's that? A friend?"

My uncle stood and stabbed a chicken leg quarter on the pan with his fork. "That's right. He's a family friend." He put the chicken on his plate and scooped a spoonful of mashed potatoes from the pot. "And he smells like pickles."

Dana burst out laughing. I couldn't stop myself

from laughing with her. My mom's face turned red.

Mr. Max raised an eyebrow. My uncle shrugged at him like he had no idea why we were laughing. "So," my uncle said to him, "what do you write?"

We helped ourselves to the food on the table. Dana swatted a spoon at me when I reached for the corn. "I'm a travel writer," Mr. Max said. "I go all over the world and write about different cities and countries." I didn't know writers could do that. I stared at him in awe.

My mom's face lit up. "Any time you come through Alabama, you can stop here for a home cooked meal." He smiled at her and nodded.

My uncle stopped chewing his food. He looked back and forth from my mom to Mr. Max. "Has anyone heard from Elan?" We looked at him, shocked. He changed the subject, but Mr. Max didn't need to know about this. "Another family friend," my uncle said to him.

My mom stared at my uncle like she wanted to burn a hole into his head. He stared right back at her. They had a way of talking to each other silently, but I didn't want to imagine what they were saying.

"We need to talk to Elan," my uncle said out loud. "We're in danger." He ate a forkful of mashed potatoes. He looked like he was happy with himself. My mom and Mr. Max weren't smiling at each other anymore.

"I can have a friend of mine install an alarm for you," Mr. Max offered. He sounded like he wanted to help. "It'll make you safer if you're worried about being robbed." I remembered the one time our house was trashed but nothing was taken. The words 'GIVE US THE FOX' were painted above the front door.

I did a double take when PJ walked across the kitchen floor toward Dana and Melissa. He was on four paws. We had instructed him to stay in the back bedroom. I suspected Fox had convinced him to come out and get a piece of chicken.

"We don't need an alarm," Dana said. She patted PJ's head. "Our cat hears everything. He'd let us know if there was a burglar." PJ walked past her and jumped into Melissa's lap.

Mr. Max scoffed. "What's he going to do? Meow loudly?"

PJ stood on his hind legs on Melissa's lap and put his front paws on the table. Whatever he was about to do wouldn't be good. "I'll karate chop the bad man," he said. "I'm a Meow Master."

Mr. Max jumped up out of his chair. It fell behind him and crashed on the floor with a loud thud. "We're leaving," he said to Melissa. His chest heaved up and down like it couldn't get enough air. "Put the cat down."

Melissa set PJ on the floor and stood. "Uncle Max," she said, "I told you about PJ." She put her hands on her head. "He really did help me with my math homework."

"Let's calm down," my mom said. "We can talk about this." She didn't take her eyes off Mr. Max.

He looked around the table at all of us. "I thought it was just a story. You know, for fun." He cleared his throat and said to Melissa, "I forbid you from coming here anymore. I have to talk to your father. Let's go. Now."

Melissa put hands in the air. "These are my friends. Don't do this." She shrugged her shoulders at me.

Mr. Max pointed to the front door. "I'm doing this for your own good. I have to protect you." He kicked his chair away.

Melissa looked at me with tears in her eyes. "I'm sorry." She pushed her chair out and followed her uncle to the front door and out of the house. I couldn't move. Did I lose a good friend? Would I ever see her outside of school again?

## SUNDAY MORNING

I sat in the back row of the church. Dana was on one side of me and Shane was on the other. His father sat in a pew at the front of the church. I couldn't believe Mr. Connors had the nerve to come to church after what he did to Fox and the other animals. I kept an eye on him.

I didn't get any sleep the night before. I kept thinking about Melissa. I remembered the first time we met in school. I didn't think I'd ever get used to her country accent, but now I didn't notice it.

I turned each time the church doors opened, hoping she was there. Fox was my best friend, but Melissa was my favorite human. I hoped her uncle changed his mind. I didn't want to lose my friend.

It didn't help that terrible things were happening that I couldn't stop. With so many animals being hunted in the forest, I couldn't protect all of them. I knew I couldn't. I was losing hope.

The church organ came to life. I didn't recognize the song being played. For months *How Great Thou Art* had been played at the beginning and end of service. Now we had a new organist because Miss Sally had arthritis and couldn't play anymore. I didn't like change.

"Brothers and sisters," the preacher said from the pulpit. "I feel in my heart that a troubled soul needs to hear this today." He raised his arms to the side of him. "The name of the Lord is a strong tower. The righteous run to it and are safe." I swear he was staring at me.

I don't remember much after that. When the collection plate got to me, I put in fifty cents. That was ten percent of my allowance. The people around me shook their heads whenever I didn't put anything in the plate. So, I came prepared.

The organist played another song I hadn't heard before when it was time to leave. When we stood, I looked for Melissa again. I knew she wasn't there, but it was still disappointing each time I looked.

As we stepped out of the aisles to leave, Shane's dad stood in front of me. I gulped. The man was as big as a house. I didn't respect him. He had kidnapped Fox and forced him to put on a show in Las Vegas. And he had tried to take away my mom's house. Now he was hurting all the animals and calling himself *The Boss*. "Jonah," he said.

I wanted to push him out of the way. "My name is Joe," I reminded him. "You're gonna pay for what you're doing. I'm gonna make sure of it." He stared at me with a blank expression. I turned from him and pushed through the crowd.

"Joe, wait up!" Shane shouted after me. He was my friend, but I couldn't be around his father. I squeezed between people to get out. I had one foot out of the foyer when the preacher grabbed my arm.

"Hi, Joe," he said. "I've been praying for you." He smiled. "Is everything okay?"

I looked through the crowd behind me. I didn't

see Mr. Connors anywhere. I felt bad for the question I needed to ask, but I had to know the answer. "How are you supposed to love your enemies when they want to hurt you?"

He put a hand on my shoulder. "That sounds impossible, doesn't it?" I was glad he understood. I nodded. "You love your mom with all your heart, don't you? You'd do anything for her." I nodded again.

"I don't think you have to love your enemies the same way," he continued. "But you should respect them as human beings. I like to think we'd push them out of the way of a moving train." I chuckled. He was right. I couldn't let anyone get hurt if there was a way for me to stop it.

"Thank you," I told him. "I understand."

Dana grabbed my hand and pulled me toward the exit. "Come on, Joe," she begged. "We have to see what my dad and Fox are doing. The big wrestling match is on TV!"

## SUNDAY AFTERNOON

Fox and my uncle were screaming at the TV when we got home. They had a big bowl of popcorn between them on the couch. The championship wrestling match between Mr. Awesome Muscles and The Millennial Kid blasted from the TV.

My mom sighed and said, "I'm gonna take a nap with PJ. There's too much testosterone in here." Fox and my uncle didn't notice her as she walked past them to her bedroom.

"I'm starving," Dana said. She punched my shoulder. "What do you have to eat?"

I put a hand on my shoulder and held it there. I'm not sure why. It's not like my shoulder was going to fall off. But it hurt. "There's some meatloaf in the fridge. YOYO." Whenever my mom wasn't there to cook, she told me to eat YOYO — You're On Your Own. That meant I had to eat leftovers.

"Whatever," Dana said. "I should've gone home." As she passed the couch to the kitchen, she stopped behind my uncle. He didn't know she was there. She shouted "BOO!" into his ear. He jumped up and spilled the bowl of popcorn all over the floor. Dana continued walking to the kitchen, laughing the whole way.

"Not funny!" my uncle shouted after her. "Grab me a drink while you're in there."

Dana kept walking. "It's not my job. You do it."

I didn't care much for wrestling, but I wanted to see what The Millennial Kid could do. He was the youngest guy in wrestling history. He wasn't covered in muscles like most of the older wrestlers. He didn't wear a mask. And he was as popular as Mr. Awesome Muscles.

Fox didn't say anything when I sat next to him. He held out his fist. I pounded it with my fist in what we called a fist pump. It wasn't hard, and it didn't hurt. It's what we did to greet each other since he couldn't shake hands.

Mr. Awesome Muscles dove from the top of a post in the ring. He flew straight for the Millennial Kid! There wasn't any hope for the Kid. Mr. Awesome Muscles was twice his size.

Mr. Awesome Muscles crushed The Millennial Kid and pinned him to the mat. The count was 1. It looked like he would stay the champion. Then the count was 2. Half of the crowd cheered for him. The other half yelled for The Millennial Kid to get up. The referee raised his hand to count to 3.

The TV shut off.

Fox and my uncle both jumped up and shouted, "No!"

My mom stepped in front of the TV. She had the remote control in her hand. "Why is there popcorn all over my floor?" She pointed down at the mess. "There's no excuse for this."

"Are you kidding me?!" Fox shouted.

"Turn it back on!" my uncle begged. He tried to snatch the remote from my mom, but she swung it over her shoulder before he could reach it. He got down on his hands and knees and threw handfuls of popcorn into the bowl as fast as he could. "This can't be happening!"

My mom handed the remote to me when my uncle finished. "I'll leave you in charge." She yawned as she walked away. "There's too much noise for me to sleep."

"Turn it on, man!" Fox shouted into my ear. I shook my head and turned it back on. None of us believed what we saw and heard on the screen.

"In the biggest upset in wrestling history," the announcer said, "the Millennial Kid has beat Mr. Awesome Muscles to win the world championship!"

Mr. Awesome Muscles shook the Kid's hand

and hugged him. He handed the Championship belt to the Kid himself. It was like he was handing the Kid his dynasty and approved of it. The crowd cheered for both of them.

The Millennial Kid put his shirt back on. He accepted the championship belt and held it high in the air. The crowd roared. "We witnessed history today!" the announcer shouted.

I turned the TV off. None of us said anything. My uncle stood and pointed at Fox. "Ha, ha, ha! My guy won!" He danced in circles like he had scored a touchdown.

Fox crossed his arms. "He cheated."

My uncle kept laughing. "No one likes a sore loser."

Dana came into the living room with a ham

sandwich in her hand. She took a bite. "What did I miss?"

"Mr. Awesome Muscles lost," my uncle said. "That means my guy won. Fox's guy lost."

Fox jumped off the couch and headed for the kitchen. "At least my hair isn't turning gray."

Dana choked and spit out a mouthful of her sandwich. My uncle put a hand on his head. It used to be completely black. Now gray hairs were sprinkled throughout it. "Gray hairs are a sign of wisdom," he explained. "That's how I knew my guy would win!"

I chuckled. I loved my family, even though they were crazy. We were honest with each other, even when it hurt. It was time to face the truth. I had to tell my mom about my report card.

**REPORT CARD**

ENGLISH ................ C

HISTORY ................ B

SCIENCE ................ B

MATH .................... B

ART ........................ A

GYM ....................... A

## SUNDAY NIGHT

I closed my bedroom door and stared at the backpack on the floor by my closet. My report card was inside of it. I had never gotten a C before. I was hard for me to breathe. I needed to take it out and show it to my mom. I owed her the truth.

I sat on my bed and considered my options. I could give it to her tomorrow after school. I wouldn't have to worry about it tonight. Or I could give it to her now and get it over with. My stomach churned.

I had called Melissa's house. She would know what to do. Her uncle answered and said she wasn't available. I wanted to ask him if he changed his mind about PJ, and if Melissa could come over. He hung up before I could do that.

My Uncle Mike and Dana had gone home for the evening. Fox and PJ chased each other around the house. My mom yelled at them to stop sometimes and laughed about it at other times. I wished I could get Fox's attention. He ate my homework once before. I wished he'd eat my report card too.

I stood and grabbed the backpack. I had an idea.

I opened the backpack and pulled out a piece of paper and a pencil. I was going to write my mom a letter telling her the truth. I wouldn't have to talk to her about my bad grade. I could apologize ahead of time in writing and promise to do better. Why didn't I think of this earlier? I'm a writer!

That's what I did for the next ten minutes. When I was done, I breathed easier. I didn't feel like the world was going to end. Don't get me wrong. My stomach was weak. But I felt like I could face the truth.

I opened my bedroom door. I smelled hamburgers cooking in the kitchen. That's where my mom would be. I clutched my letter and report card, took a deep breath, and headed for the kitchen.

"I hope you're hungry," my mom said from the kitchen counter. "I added extra garlic to your burgers, the way you like it." She winked at me.

I gulped. I set the report card on the table first then the letter on top of it. I hoped my plan worked.

If she saw the report card first, then I had a lot of explaining to do.

"What do you have there?" my mom asked, smiling.

I walked over to the oven behind her and grabbed the spatula on the counter. "I'll flip the burgers." My back was to her. "I need you to read the letter on the table."

She crossed her arms. It was probably my imagination, but she seemed angry already. She said, "Okay, Jonah." I turned and watched her walk to the table. She moved slowly, like she was afraid of what she'd find.

The hamburgers sizzled. I flipped them so they wouldn't burn. When I looked back at my mom, she set the letter down and picked up the report card. I was dizzy again.

I focused on the hamburgers and moved them an inch in every direction. The sizzling was so loud I thought I was going to go deaf. The smell was so strong I couldn't breathe. My throat was tight. I couldn't swallow.

I jumped when my mom grabbed the spatula. "That's enough, Jonah. They're done." Her expression was blank. I couldn't tell what she was thinking or how angry she was. Would I be grounded for the rest of my life?

"Look at me, Jonah," she said. I couldn't stop staring at the hamburgers. My mom grabbed the pan and turned off the burner. She set the pan on the counter. My fingers trembled. She sighed.

"A lot has happened this year," she said. "We left our friends behind when we moved here." I missed my friends in Orlando, but I wouldn't have met Fox if we hadn't moved. "The IRS wanted to take this house away from us." Thank goodness we still had it.

Fox and PJ raced into the kitchen and ran in circles around us. My mom put a hand on her forehead. "And plenty of unexpected changes." Fox and PJ ran back into the living room. My mom and I both chuckled.

"One thing will never change," she said. "You'll

always be my son and I'll always love you, no matter what." She put her arms around me and squeezed tight. "I don't want you to feel like you can't talk to me. You'll get through this and do better next time."

I shivered and cried. I was relieved but felt guilty for hiding this from my mom. "I'm sorry, mom. I'm supposed to be smart. I don't know what happened."

She held me at arm's length. "Listen to me, Jonah. You are smart. You passed your classes, and you've always done well." She walked back to the kitchen table and grabbed the report card. "This doesn't define you. You don't always have to be the best." She set it down. "I just ask that you do your best."

I promised her I would. I wasn't sure if it would happen in the next day. I had to reveal my clay project to the art class. I could tell the class what it was, but I didn't know if anyone would understand why I made it.

## MONDAY MORNING

When I walked into school that morning, I held my breath. I didn't know how to act around Melissa when I saw her. I didn't know if she was allowed to talk to me. I wanted to talk to her more than anything.

"Are you okay?" Shane asked when I passed him in the halls later. I remembered the first time I met him in this same hall and he shoved me to the floor. I never thought we'd be friends.

"Not really," I said.

He stopped me. "What's up? You raced out of church yesterday."

Kids passed us on both sides. A few bumped into me. None of them apologized. "Your dad…the animals…Melissa." The class bells rang. I shrugged at Shane. "We'll talk after school." I headed for the art room. It was time to face Melissa.

"Hi, Joe!" Melissa shouted when I stepped in the room. She waved for me to join her at her table.

"Stop shouting!" Miss Pendleton yelled. "That just burns me up!"

I met Melissa at her table. She smiled at me. I smiled back. "I called my dad and told him what happened," she said. "I told him how PJ did my math homework for me that one time." She chuckled. "He was silent for a long time, but then he asked to speak to my uncle."

"I'm guessing it was good news," I said. Her dad must have told her uncle that we could still be friends. I was glad. I took a deep breath and relaxed.

Miss Pendleton knocked a fist on our table like she was knocking on a door. "Since you like to talk so much, your table can go first." Our clay projects were laid out in front of us. She had taken them out of the kiln that morning.

"Wait!" Sam shouted. "Let me go first!" He held his project over his head. "My project is dope!"

Miss Pendleton rolled her eyes. "Go ahead. This should be fun."

"Ladies and gentlemen," Sam said, standing at his table. "I present to you — Professor Mug!" He held his clay mug out. It didn't look special. It was a big cup that was uneven and without a handle.

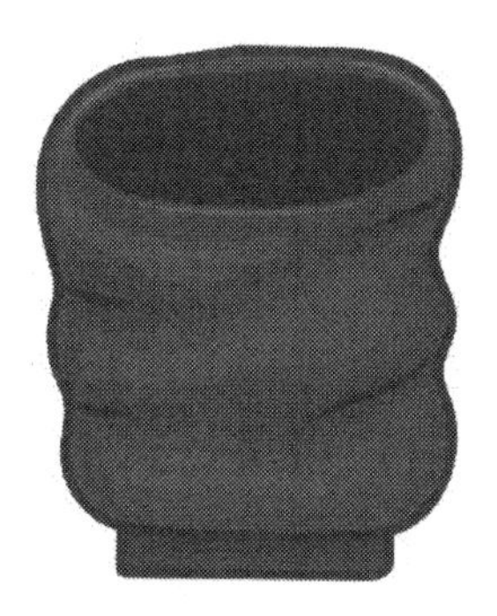

He turned the mug around. The class burst out laughing. The other side of the mug had two big eyeballs and a long tongue sticking out of it.

"Professor Mug is the worst teacher there is," Sam continued, shaking his head. "He doesn't say anything." Sam looked around the class and nodded at each of us. "His mouth is always full of clay."

I couldn't hold it in. I laughed and laughed and laughed! His mouth was full of clay? His mouth was made of clay!

"I could have been a doctor," Miss Pendleton muttered. "Fifty years…I've wasted fifty years." She rubbed her temples. "Melissa, you're up. It can't get any worse."

I nudged Melissa to let her know it would be okay. She nodded. She picked up her clay flower pot from the table. "This is my flower pot. I made sure it's big enough to hold dozens of flowers." She shrugged like there was nothing else to say.

"It's for her dad!" Sam reminded the class. "Her dad likes flowers!" He laughed. Some kids chuckled with him. The others were silent. They were scared to show their projects to the class.

"My mom was in the hospital for a long time," Melissa said to Sam. "My dad and I took her fresh roses every day." She didn't say anything after that. She couldn't. I helped her set the pot back on the table.

"This is how they remember her," I told Sam. He didn't laugh any more. He turned his head from me.

"Okay," Miss Pendleton said. "Jonah, you're up."

I grabbed my project from the table and held it up. It wasn't perfect, but it was the best I could do. Before I could say anything, Sam mumbled, "Nice bowl." It looked like a large salad bowl and I could have told them that's what it was.

I flipped the project over and put it on top of my head. It fit perfectly. Two sides were longer than the rest to cover my ears. The front covered my eyebrows. The back covered the top half of my head.

"Sometimes life is scary," I said. "We're afraid." I remembered my first day at this school. "It's easier if we cover our heads and protect ourselves. That way no one can hurt us." I took the helmet off and set it on the table. I hadn't planned what I said next.

"We don't need a helmet. What we need are our friends and family to remind us that we're stronger together. And we'll always be safe." I looked at Melissa and smiled. She smiled back.

The rest of the kids presented their clay projects one by one. My favorite was a volcano. Terry had spread a packet of ketchup from the cafeteria on the sides of it. The worst one was a little blob Nicole called a rock. I don't think she put any effort into it.

Sam made sure to stop by Miss Pendleton's desk when class was over. He held up his mug to her, eyeballs and tongue facing her. "Professor Mug says 'Give Sam an A! He did good with clay!'"

"Fifty years," Miss Pendleton muttered again. "Fifty years."

I felt a lot better when I left school that day. Melissa and I would be okay. The clay project was done. I didn't have anything to hide from my mom. Life was good.

If only I had known I was going to face my greatest fear when I got home.

## MONDAY AFTERNOON

I couldn't believe my eyes when I walked into my house. The two men I had seen watching me in the park were standing in the living room with their hands in their pockets. One was dressed in a blue suit and the other in a black and red suit. My mom was talking to them and laughing. I wanted to tell her to run.

"Jonah," my mom said when she saw me, "come over here for a minute." She waved for me to join them. I wished my Uncle Mike was there. He had dropped me off to take Dana home because she wasn't feeling well.

I walked over cautiously. I didn't trust the men.

"This is Mr. Thompson and Mr. Pool," she said, pointing at them. I suspected their first names were Billy and John, the hunters. "They're new in town and looking for a place to stay. They may move across the street into the Hunters' old house." Mr. and Mrs. Hunter had moved up north to live in their vacation home. I missed them. They had bought all my chocolate when we first moved here.

"Also," my mom continued, "Miss Julie brought a young skunk named Stinky by. She said your best friend would know the best place to release him." I nodded. Stinky and Fox had been friends in the forest.

Both men stood and faced me. "Nice to meet you, Jonah," the one called Mr. Thompson said. He reached out a hand for me to shake it.

"My name is…" There was a knock on the front door. "I'll get it." I needed a distraction.

It only got worse when I opened the door. Shane's dad was on the other side, smoking a cigar, and staring at me. It was like the first time I met him, when he had threatened to take away our house.

"What are you doing here?" was all I could say. Did he come to gloat? Were these his henchmen in our living room? They were on a sick mission to destroy all the animals. I knew he was The Boss. I didn't know if there was any way to stop him.

Shane stepped up from behind Mr. Connors. "Hear him out, Joe. He's not here to hurt anyone." His hands were clasped like he was begging me.

I crossed my arms. I didn't want to hear anything Mr. Connors had to say. It could all be lies and threats. That was all he ever said to us.

He pulled the cigar out of his mouth. "It will only take a minute, Joe. You don't ever have to see me again after this."

I doubted it was true. I looked back at my mom and considered getting her attention. She was still talking and laughing with the two men sitting on our couch now. They didn't look dangerous. "Go ahead," I told Mr. Connors.

He cleared his throat. "I've made a lot of mistakes. I've hurt a lot of people. I hurt you. I hurt the fox." He put a hand in his pocket. "It was wrong. I was wrong." He looked me in the eyes. "I can't make up for what I've done. But I'll spend the rest of my life trying to."

His shoulders sunk. I wanted to believe he was telling the truth, but how could I? The Boss stood in front of me, lying to my face. He had hurt my best friend in the past and he was hurting the other animals now.

"He's telling the truth," Shane said. "His sponsor told me how much he's changed." I huffed. "I'm serious," Shane continued. "My father is donating his time and money to help others."

I was confused. None of this made sense. I looked at Mr. Connors. "Call it off. Stop the hunters." I pointed to the men on the couch. "You know who they are. Get them out of here."

Mr. Connors — The Boss — glanced at the men on the couch. He shrugged and put his hands in the air. "I don't know what you're talking about. And I have no idea who those men are."

As much as I didn't want to believe him, his eyes told me what I needed to know. He was telling the truth. He was not The Boss.

Was I dreaming? He wasn't The Boss? The men on our couch weren't the hunters? Was there a boss? Were there hunters? Living in a world with talking animals was driving me crazy. I needed to lay down.

"Are you okay?" Shane asked.

I nodded. "I'll call you later." I turned to Mr. Connors. His face was drawn like he was exhausted and weak. He was truly sorry. All I could do was whisper, "Thank you."

Shane grabbed his dad's arm and pulled him toward the driveway. "Call me, Joe," he said. And then they were gone.

I closed the door and turned around. What I saw made me more scared than I had been in my entire life.

Mr. Thompson was standing behind my mom with one hand around her waist and the other over her mouth. She had tears in her eyes.

"Mom!" I shouted.

"Tell us where the fox is," Mr. Pool said. He stood over the couch and straightened his clothes. He spoke slowly and clearly. "Don't make us hurt your mom."

I thought as fast as I could. They couldn't hurt my mom! I wouldn't let them! I was strong, and I was fast. Was this the reason the land had given me these powers? The men weren't close enough together though. I could stop one, but I couldn't stop both at the same time. I wished Shane would come back.

I saw beautiful blue eyes peer from the bedroom door down the hallway. It was Fox. I wanted to tell him not to come out. But I knew who he was. He would sacrifice himself to save my mom.

"He doesn't live here," I told the men. "The law doesn't allow it." The bedroom door opened wider and PJ stepped out on four paws. He walked toward the living room. What was he doing?

"Maybe not," Mr. Thompson said. "But you know where to find him." He stepped over to Mr. Pool's side. "Your mom wouldn't tell us. But you will when we hurt her."

PJ entered the living room. He walked over to Mr. Thompson, rubbed his sides against his legs, and purred. Then he sat in front of him and smiled.

"Get away from me!" Mr. Thompson shouted. He bent down and kicked PJ halfway across the room. PJ landed on his feet. Mr. Thompson stared at him. "Your eyes… they're blue. You're one of them."

Fox raced out of the bedroom and stopped in front of my mom and the bad guys. He stood on his hind legs. "Take me," he said. "Leave them alone."

No. This couldn't be happening. There had to be a better way. I was tired of my friends and family getting hurt. I was tired of Fox sacrificing himself for us. I had to do something.

"Now!" Fox shouted. PJ raced toward the bad guys and ran in a circle around them and my mom. Fox chased after PJ, like he had the day before. They ran faster and faster in circles around them. Mr. Thompson reached out for them, but they were too fast.

Fox and PJ finally stopped, huffing. Fox was back in front of them and PJ was behind them. "I've got you now," Mr. Thompson said. He reached down to grab Fox by his neck.

"Karate chop!" PJ yelled. He threw a paw into the back of Mr. Thompson's leg then twisted and threw the same paw into the back of Mr. Pool's leg. They both fell to their knees.

My mom broke free and ran over to me. She wrapped her arms around me and pulled me toward the door.

"Now, Stinky!" Fox yelled. The skunk ran out of the bedroom and stood in front of the bad guys.

"Hey," Mr. Pool said to Mr. Thompson. "Isn't that the skunk from the forest? The one that sprayed us?"

"At your service," Stinky said. He turned

around, balanced himself on his front paws and raised his rump into the air.

"No!" Mr. Thompson shouted. "Not again!"

Liquid shot out of Stinky's rear end like a water hose. He waved his rump back and forth from Mr. Pool's face to Mr. Thompson's face. There was so much stinky skunk spray that it didn't look like it would ever end.

"It smells so bad!" Mr. Pool shouted. "I can't breathe!"

"My eyes!" Mr. Thompson screamed. "It's burning my eyes!"

They jumped up, scratching at their faces and eyes. My mom pushed me behind her and opened the front door. "Get out!" she yelled. They stumbled over themselves and raced out the door. My mom pulled her cell phone out of her purse and took a picture of their license plate.

She closed the front door and locked it. She hugged me close. "Thank goodness you're safe," she said. She dialed 911, put the phone to her ear, and walked in circles.

"Not bad, huh?" PJ said. He stood on his hind legs with Fox and Stinky next to him. "I've got moves."

I patted his head. I'm glad he was there. I put my palms together in a praying position and bowed to him. "You are a Meow Master."

"You did ok," Fox said. "For a cat." He laughed and patted PJ on the shoulder.

I patted Fox's head too. "You were willing to give yourself up for my mom. That's amazing, Fox. Thank you." He blushed and swatted a paw like it was nothing.

"What about me?" Stinky asked. "I helped."

I rubbed his head, making sure to stay away from his backside. "You saved the day," I told him. "We couldn't have done this without you. We are forever your friends." He had the biggest smile a skunk could make.

"What do we do now?" PJ asked. "The bad guys are out there."

I hadn't thought that far ahead. My mom had a picture of the bad guys' car. She gave that information to the police on the phone. In the best-case scenario, the bad guys would be caught that night. "We prepare ourselves," I said. "We don't know what's coming next."

I thought I had the answers. But it turned out I didn't have any of them. I had no idea who The Boss was. I hated to think it was someone I knew. Why were they determined to hurt me and my friends?

I would have all the answers before the night was over.

## MONDAY EVENING

Two policemen came and took statements from me and my mom. It was hard explaining to them what happened. We couldn't say anything about Fox, PJ, or Stinky. My mom told them two men broke into our house. She sprayed them with pepper spray and they ran off. It wasn't 100% the truth, but it was close enough that the cops could look for the bad guys. I agreed with everything she said.

Right as the cops were leaving, the American Indian Elan came into our house. He shook my hand right away. "How are you doing, Joe?"

I was relieved to see him. He was our best chance in saving the animals in the forest. He was the last member of his tribe, The Talking Dragons. He was the only one who understood why some of the animals had blue eyes and the ability to walk and talk like humans.

"It's been rough," I admitted. "Have you seen Miss Julie?"

He nodded. "I stopped by the wildlife sanctuary. We'll save as many as we can." He put a hand on my shoulder. "How about you? Have you noticed any changes?"

He was referring to my blue eyes and how they affected me. For whatever reason, the land had chosen me to protect it. Elan was fascinated by this because the land had always chosen animals. I wasn't sure where I fit in, though. I was faster and stronger than before I had the blue eyes. But I hadn't done anything with it yet.

I shook my head.

"Elan," my mom said, "it's good to see you." She gave him a shoulder hug. "I'm glad you're here."

A man I didn't know stepped into the house and stood next to Elan. He had caramel colored skin like Elan and was the same height. He looked just like Elan but had a short beard and mustache. "This is my brother, Waya," Elan said.

"Nice to meet you, Waya," my mom said, shaking his hand. "I'm Julie." She pointed to me. "This is my son, Jonah."

I shook my head. How many times did we have to do this? "Please call me Joe," I said.

Waya chuckled. "Hello, Joe. Elan has told me a lot about you." Elan shrugged like he was sorry. "I'm very happy to know you."

"Elan," my mom said, "You said you were the last member of your tribe. I'm confused."

Waya put his hands out and said, "It's true. My brother and I are the last of The Talking Dragons." That didn't make any sense. If there were two in the tribe, how could one be the last? "I didn't believe in what The Talking Dragons stand for and left the tribe many years ago." He pulled out his wallet and handed me a card. "I'm a record producer in Los Angeles now."

"He lost his way," Elan said, wrapping an arm around his brother. "But he's coming back."

"Elan has been writing me letters for the past year," Waya said. "Crazy talk about how he found the land of our ancestors. How he found a talking fox." He shook his head like he couldn't believe it. "But then I saw a video on the internet with a talking fox and a boy — you." He nodded at me. Thanks a lot, Shane. "I had to see it with my own eyes."

PJ walked into the room on four paws and looked at Waya. "There's my favorite cat," Elan said. He pointed to Waya. "This is my brother. Show him what you can do."

PJ looked over at me. His eyes were darker. I sensed he was scared. He turned around and walked out of the living room.

"What was that about?" Elan asked. "PJ loves to talk about himself."

My mom shrugged. "It's been a long day. He's tired."

"Can we see the fox?" Waya asked. "It will prove to me once for all that my ancestors were right. This is sacred land that must be protected."

I waved at him. "Follow me. Fox took a skunk named Stinky back to his home in the forest earlier. Fox is saying his goodbyes." I walked into the kitchen and to the back door. I held it open and let the others out first.

PJ stopped me before I went outside and joined them. "What's wrong?" I asked him. It was weird how he walked away from us without saying a word.

"It's here," PJ said. "The darkness." He stood and put a paw on my leg. "You can't sense it?" Nothing was out of the ordinary. I shook my head.

"Did he ask to see Fox?" PJ asked.

"Yeah," I said. "He's Elan's brother. He's from the tribe sworn to protect Fox and all animals that walk and talk." I scratched his head. "We were chosen, PJ. You, me, Fox, and Stinky."

PJ tapped my leg three times. "His name is Waya. Do you know what that means?" I shook my head. "Waya means 'wolf'."

My mom shouted from the backyard, "Come on, Jonah!"

I took PJ's paw off my leg so his four paws were on the floor. "I don't know what you're getting at," I told him. "Your name is PJ, which we shortened from Peanut Butter Jelly. We still love you." I stepped outside and reached to pull the door closed.

"Wolves attack red foxes," PJ said before I closed it. I ignored him. Waya was probably the name Elan's brother was given when he was born.

I walked past the outhouse and toward the chicken coop. It didn't look like Fox had returned yet. My mom, Elan, and Waya were standing by the fence when I joined them.

"Their powers came from this land," Elan said to his brother. He motioned around us. "This is where our ancestors lived and thrived."

Waya turned to me. "The fox was the first one in this generation to have the power. It started with him. Where is he?"

I shrugged. "He's disappeared for months at a time before." I felt like I had to explain further. "His parents are out there." My mom nodded.

Elan turned his head from side to side. "Does anyone else smell smoke?" We sniffed the air but none of us smelled anything.

Waya sighed. "If a man wanted to destroy all the animals, it wouldn't do any good to hunt them. This forest is way too big for that." He turned and looked at me. "It would be quicker to burn the forest down."

"Don't say stuff like that," my mom warned. "I don't want to imagine anyone is that sick." She leaned against the fence. "It would burn down the houses around it, including mine."

"I didn't mean to upset you," Waya said. He faced Elan. "We should get going. We can come back tomorrow, if that's okay." My mom nodded.

"It was nice to meet you, Joe," he said to me. "I'm sure we'll see a lot more of each other." He shook my hand again and studied my eyes. "Amazing."

"Come on, big brother," Elan said. "We'll get some fast food on the way home."

"No way," Waya said. "Let's go to a steak house. I'm paying."

Elan chuckled. "If you insist. You're the boss."

"That's right," Waya said. He winked at me. "I'm The Boss."

Oh, no! Will Waya burn the forest down??? Why??? Will Joe learn how to use his powers??? Find out what happens to Fox and all the animals in the forest in 2019! Be sure to follow my author page (David Blaze) on Amazon.com and like my Facebook page for all updates (links provided on the next page). This is the 6th book in the My Fox world. Start with My Fox Begins to learn how all of this started!

AVAILABLE AT AMAZON.COM
Print and Ebook

Don't miss these other books from David Blaze!

For younger children!

For Christmas!

You can keep up with everything I'm doing at:

www.davidblazebooks.com

Be sure to click the Follow button next to my name (David Blaze) on Amazon.com to be notified when my new books are released.

And you can follow me on Facebook. Just search for David Blaze, Children's Author. Be sure to like the page! I will be doing live giveaways of future ebooks and paperback books on that page.

If you enjoyed my story, please tell your friends and family. I'd also appreciate it if you'd leave a review on Amazon.com and tell me what you think about my best friend, Fox.

See you soon!

Made in the USA
Columbia, SC
19 November 2019